The Wife of Pilate

By Gertrud von le Fort

SIMPLY and profoundly, Gertrud von le Fort tells the unforgettable story of Claudia Procula, Pilate's wife. In a vivid dream of early morning — and those, she is convinced, are the dreams which always come true — Claudia sees herself running through a series of rooms, crowded with people at prayer. Through each room reverberate the words: ". . . suffered under Pontius Pilate, was crucified, died, and was buried." The impact of the dream and the events which follow it are told by Miss von le Fort with consummate beauty and depth. Here is a book which readers will find truly absorbing, written by one of the most distinguished authors and intellectuals of our time.

The Wife of Pilate

The Wife of Pilate

Gertrud von le Fort

TRANSLATED BY

MARIE C. BUEHRLE

THE BRUCE PUBLISHING COMPANY
MILWAUKEE

A translation from the German, *Die Frau des Pilatus,* by
Gertrud von le Fort, Insel-Verlag, Wiesbaden, Germany.

Rosary College Dewey Classification Number: 833.91
Library of Congress Catalog Card Number: 57–10826
© 1957 by The Bruce Publishing Company
MADE IN THE UNITED STATES OF AMERICA

(2/57)

The Wife of Pilate

The Wife of Pilate

FROM ROME, THE GREEK FREEWOMAN, PRAXEDIS TO JULIA, WIFE OF DECIUS GALLICUS IN VIENNA:

Revered Lady, I have just had the news that within the next few days the legion of Quintus Crassus will be transferred from Rome to Gaul and hasten, therefore, to entrust to one of the tribunes this complete account, which your sisterly love for my dear mistress has prompted you to request of me. In my first report, I was apparently unable to make things sufficiently clear to you. I beg of you to pardon my confusion — when last I wrote I was still too profoundly affected by the appalling events. Besides, there were doubts as to the trustworthiness of my messenger at the time, and the wave of persecution, as you know, had not fully abated. In the meantime, the perilous situation has improved. The messenger whom I have chosen, although not one of your faith, is nevertheless discreet and free from prejudice, a sober Roman who with cool deliberation disapproves of the persecution. Today therefore, I can freely confide everything to you.

According to what you tell me, the report still persists in Gaul that the Procurator, after wandering in despair from place to place, sought and found his death in the mountains of Switzerland. I need not correct this legend since you know that it rests upon an invention. Not the Procurator, but his wife, my beloved Lady Claudia Procula, has, as it were, wandered throughout the reaches of the world. I say as it were, for there are also spiritual reaches which not only denote the world, but in a higher sense are the world in its reality. I shall therefore begin with my Lady's astonishing dream which you rightly suspect as the root of her destiny. I also agree with you entirely when you distinguish between dreams and dreams; for there are some that at the outset bear the aspect of a compelling truth even when no divining priest is at hand to assure us of it. And while ordinary dreams flit by, agile and fleet of foot like children playing hide and seek, these others to which you refer rise before us at their very beginning, distinct as the awe-inspiring, sculptured columns of the Roman forum which to him who looks upon them seem to cry out: "Do not ever forget us!" And to these latter dreams belongs the one of which we are speaking.

Although decades of years have passed, I still re-member accurately all the circumstances that accom-panied it. At that time my youthful mistress was fre-quently depressed because she believed herself neg-lected by her husband. Like a spoilt child she had, as you know, an exacting idea of what a husband's love should be. It is true that in those days the Procurator left her much alone; but probably it was only because of the burden of his office, associated as it was with a thousand annoyances from a small but extremely difficult nation, the government of which had become utterly irksome to him. On the morning of which I am speaking, however, my mistress was radiant with joy and rapture, because the Procurator had spent the night with her.

"O my Praxedis," she called out to me, "Eros has been gracious to me after all! This night I have been loved for my whole life." Tenderly her glance sought the little statue of the god of love with which the Procurator had adorned her room.

"No, I do not wish to get up yet." She warded me off when I was preparing to help her to dress. "Let me rest a while longer and dream; for in spirit I am still lying in my husband's arms." She permitted me

9

to straighten her pillows, and smiling contentedly settled into them like a tired child.

Suddenly while I was in the atrium arranging the flowers and fruits for the table — I had sent the chattering slave girls away so that no one might disturb my mistress in her sleep — I heard her frightened cry. When I entered the room, she was sitting on her bed staring at me with large, agitated eyes. It was as though the sweet satiety of happiness had been wiped away from her beautiful childlike face and the shadows of many a coming year had fallen over its youthfulness; or else she seemed to have met in visible form some inexorable fate decreed by the gods. Her arms strained toward me, then dropped as though lamed.

"For me all happiness is now at an end," she said. "I have had such a bad dream — and you know, my Praxedis, that the dreams of early morning are dreams that are true!"

I begged her to tell me what she had seen in her dream; perhaps after all I could give it some favorable interpretation. Slowly, her fluency of speech returned. "I found myself in a dim room," she began, "where a great number of people were assembled and appeared to be praying; but their words passed by me like murmuring water. Then suddenly it seemed as though my ears opened wide or as though the jet of a fountain were leaping from dark waters, and I heard distinctly the words: 'Suffered under Pontius Pilate, was crucified, died, and was buried.' I could not explain it to myself how my husband's name had come to be upon the lips of these people, nor what it might mean. Nevertheless I felt an undefined dread upon hearing these words, as though they could have no other but some mysterious and ominous significance.

"Bewildered, I wanted to leave the place, but already found myself in a still darker room, one which reminded me of the cemeteries outside the gates of Rome. It was even more thronged than the other, with people praying, and here too I heard the startling words: 'Suffered under Pontius Pilate, was crucified, died, and was buried.' I tried to escape into the open air; but found myself again in a closed room, this time one with a sacred aspect. People were assembled praying, and again I heard my husband's name. I hurried on. Room after room opened at my approach. Occasionally I thought that I recognized one of the familiar temples of Rome, although strangely altered. I saw marble pulpits with stone inlays of red and gold; but

11

not a single image of gods that I knew. In the apses, large strange mosaics frequently emerged, representing as it seemed, some God in the character of a judge with whom I was unacquainted. Before I could properly grasp the meaning of His face, the terrible words: 'Suffered under Pontius Pilate, was crucified, died, and was buried' were on the lips of a closely pressed multitude and went through me like a chill. . . .

"Farther and farther I ran, through castellated gates, and passed with hurrying feet through many a stern and solemn basilica. Ever greater seemed the number of people gathered together, ever more strange the architecture of their churches, until suddenly the weighty porches began to rise, and as though freed from all the laws of stone, they floated lightly toward heaven. The praying ceased; but invisible choirs were singing and from these also my husband's name came echoing toward me: 'Crucified under Pontius Pilate, died, and was buried.'

"Then the ethereal porches also vanished, familiar columns rose into view, adorned however, with rare draperies, and all but crushed under their magnificence. Great volumes of music came streaming through the halls within the columns: strange choirs of manifold

12

voices mingling and separating so that the words flowed unintelligibly into one another. But suddenly from out of the tossing waves of sound, a single voice arose, direct, austere, flawlessly distinct. Accusingly, almost like a threat, the words re-echoed: 'Crucified for us, under Pontius Pilate . . .'

"I ran, I ran as though hounded by furies; farther ever farther. It seemed to me as though I had hurried through centuries and must hurry through centuries more, spurred on to the end of time, pursued by that dearest of names as though it concealed a destiny, immeasurably heavy, threatening to shadow not only his precious life, but that of the entire human race." She stopped; for some time we could hear a confusion of excited voices coming from outdoors. The Procurator's name beat upon our ears, and following immediately upon it, like a mysterious transformation of the dream voice, the many-throated cry: "Crucify Him, crucify Him!"

We knew the ways of this fanatic little nation with which we were condemned to live, we had grown accustomed to the ridiculous street scenes staged for us from time to time when the ambitious priestly caste was bent upon forcing its obstinate demands upon the

13

Procurator. Ordinarily we paid but little attention to these demonstrations. Today, however, it seemed to me as though something out in the street was attuned to the dream which my mistress had just related. The distant centuries through which her dream had carried her shrank in fright back into the present which was preparing to confirm what she had seen. A glance at her face, grown deadly pale, told me that she was having the same thought.

In order to quiet her, I summoned one of the slave girls standing ready in the atrium, who are known always to be informed concerning the news of the city, and I asked her what was happening. She told us that the Jews had dragged a man before the tribunal whom they accused of wishing to make himself king, and they demanded that the Procurator have him crucified. They were a bad, ungrateful people, she said; for this Jesus of Nazareth, as the prisoner is called, had done many good things. He was a great worker of miracles and a healer of the sick. She wanted to go on with her story, but I gave her a sign to stop; for I noticed that my mistress was becoming more and more agitated at her words.

"O I knew it," she cried when we were alone, "that

14

the dreams of the early morning are true. Through this prisoner my dream will fulfill itself. The Procurator dare not condemn Him! Go to him, good Praxedis, and beg him in the name of all my affection to set the accused man free. Hurry! For the sake of all the gods, hurry!"

I hesitated; but not for fear of my task. Our master was a courteous gentleman and I shall never forget the relaxed, casual way in which he had pronounced me a freewoman the moment he learned that I was a Greek; but in official affairs he did not listen to women. I reminded my mistress of this; but she persisted: "Today he will listen to me; for last night he loved me."

Thereupon I discarded my doubts and went over to that part of the palace known as the Hall of Justice. The centurion on duty led me to the Procurator. The latter, although much older than his wife, looked very youthful on that morning, with his impressive figure, his strong chin and narrow, controlled mouth. He was just returning from his bath, clothed in a clean toga, preparing to go out to the turbulent people. It is one of the innumerable oddities of the Jews that they believe themselves defiled if they enter our houses.

I delivered my message. He listened to me calmly

15

and no look upon his restrained face indicated that he was in a hurry. Had I spoken for a half hour, I do not believe that he would have interrupted me. In fact, it seemed to suit him very well to let the unruly multitude wait outside. You know, my Lady, that sometimes he could in a silent way be malicious toward this people.

"Very well, Praxedis; I thank your mistress, greet her for me," he answered finally, and although his face — Oh! those impenetrable Roman faces — betrayed nothing of what he thought concerning my message, I had a definite impression that it was not unwelcome to him; rather as though it were a confirmation of his own opinion about the prisoner. I hurried back to my mistress and told her that the Procurator had listened to me graciously. This seemed to quiet her somewhat. She permitted me to dress her and even used freely the numerous cosmetics upon which, despite her blooming youth, she set great store. We then went over to the triclinium where we could not hear the continuous tumult of the people. I read to her, a few Greek love poems which she specially liked because they reflected the emotions that she was accustomed to require from her husband.

16

Suddenly the slave-girl whom we had questioned about the turmoil in the street came rushing into the room. "O Mistress," she cried, "your husband is letting the prisoner be crucified after all, and His friends believed firmly that God's angels would come to His aid." My mistress fairly flew from her chair and out of the room. I followed, but failed to overtake her until we both stood out on the flat roof over the low fore part of the palace, leaning over the wall from which we could look over the entire square below the Hall of Justice.

The Procurator with gloomy face was sitting upon the judgment seat. Evidently he had already passed sentence; for the legionaries were laying hands upon the prisoner standing before him, who was clothed in the tatters of a red soldier-cloak and wore a crown of twisted thorns around His bleeding head. But the really heart-rending thing to see was that this pitiable One looked as though He were having pity upon the whole world, even upon the Procurator, His judge — yes, even upon him!

This compassion completely enveloped the face of the condemned, and if my life depended upon it I could not describe it other than to say that the face

17

wore this expression of an unbounded, an altogether incredible pity at sight of which a strange dizziness lay hold of me. It seemed to me as though this compassion, transforming as it did the face of the prisoner beyond recognition, must needs annihilate the whole world that I knew. Indeed, the impression that somehow my entire world had begun to totter, was so overwhelming that my resistance awakened in defiance of this tremendous power. I felt a hopeless defense rising stark within me. Motionless, helpless, yet persistent, I was clinging to my condemned world. All this transpired in a single instant; for the next moment the legionaries were already dragging the condemned away, to lead Him to His crucifixion. The Procurator rose from his judgment seat and with the look of gloom still unchanged upon his face, withdrew into the palace.

What had happened? What caused this change of attitude? We learned later that the bloodthirsty multitude had upbraided him with the reproach that he would neglect the interests of Caesar if he refused to yield. I know, noble Julia, that for this reason your coreligionists accuse him of selfish ambition. This, however, is to judge a little rashly. The Procurator, to be sure, did sacrifice a man who was innocent and he knew it; but has Rome ever hesitated to condemn the innocent if the peace of any part of the empire was at stake? The whole situation in the East was extremely tense at the time and probably every Roman would have acted in the same manner as did the Procurator. Furthermore, what does the life of one person mean to a Roman? And our master was a Roman through and through. He already belonged to that later generation which only out of a certain courtesy to ancestors, still sacrificed to the gods. For him there was in reality but one sanctuary and one place of sacrifice, Imperial Rome of the divine Emperor.

I then begged my mistress to let me take her back to her apartments. She stood as though struck by lightning, as though she herself, not the Jewish Healer, had been condemned to death. When I spoke to her she pressed her hands to her face and cried long, intensely, hopelessly; but in complete silence. She was silent also when in the course of the day a strange, inexplicable darkness spread over the land, and while everyone else in the palace was running about in terrified confusion, she seemed to sink into the dark, and cling to it as to something that responded profoundly to her own feelings.

19

Even later, she never expressed herself concerning the occurrence of that day. This gradually began to surprise me; for I was accustomed to the childlike fashion in which she confided all her feelings and experiences to me. This was the first time I stood face to face with her reserve and consequently for a long time failed to realize that the look on the face of the Man unjustly condemned had wounded and changed her for all time. And yet, His glance had not fallen upon her. It was directed exclusively toward her husband; but precisely because of this she had been struck by it; and that of which her hitherto childlike, self-seeking love had now become capable, manifested itself.

Today I know that she took his guilt upon herself, not in the least consciously or deliberately; but simply as the outpouring of a love that had broken through its customary boundaries. From then on she was sad, while he enjoyed life; she suffered while he obviously was content. Finally she even endured it that he became estranged from her, because he no longer understood her. I began to have a presentiment of the transformation of her whole being when her child came dead into the world without complaint on her part. It was just as though she were inwardly prepared for this blow as she had been for the darkness over the earth; and she accepted it patiently, though with grief.

When as a comfort I reminded her that with her youth she might hope for many more children, she seemed not to hear. As a matter of fact it was never given her to expect a second child, although she always received her husband with great tenderness. Now, however, she waited without impatience when he did not come; and an affectionate, a very quiet resignation, at times something akin to pain, was in her embrace. Now and then when she looked at him with her large, innocent eyes, inadvertently I had to think of his unjust judicial sentence, and for a moment I would find myself tempted to believe that the image of the Man he had condemned thrust itself between them. That was not true, however, if only for the reason that the Procurator to all appearances no longer thought of the incident.

Since he was soon afterward recalled to Rome, his memories of Judea seemed to be completely obliterated. The Emperor overwhelmed him with honorable commissions, and he was grateful for these distinctions. My mistress was also accepted in Rome as befitted her rank and the position of her husband; but strangely enough Rome was no longer accepted by her. In Jerusalem, she had longed to return to Rome; now it almost seemed as though she wished herself back in Jerusalem. The frenzied feasts of the world-capital which had once enchanted her, repelled her now. Her eyes filled with tears when she heard of the ill treatment of a slave. During the triumphal processions of victorious generals, in which the entire populace jubilantly participated, she trembled for the fate of the captive barbarian princes who at the end of the celebration would be put to death on the Capitoline. But the public games shook her with special horror; dying gladiators, even wild animals set upon one another for the amusement of the people, were an affliction and a torture to her. Every time that she had to accompany her husband to the Circus she trembled.

He had at the time become specially enthusiastic for the splendid spectacle of the chariot races and was seized with the ambition himself to drive a so-called quadriga or chariot. To achieve this he spent days taking hot baths by means of which with the aid of all sorts of exercises he might reduce the overweight, to which he was naturally inclined. In his ambition he even went so far as to have his favorite slave instructed in the occult arts of one of those magicians who, as the people believed, were able, by certain excessively cruel sacrifices to the demons, to grant victories in the Circus. For the enlightened mind of our master, this was surely strange conduct. I myself could not restrain a smile at this contradiction, and I believe that I detected the same on the sly face of the slave; but Claudia did not smile when she heard of it. On the contrary, it only increased her aversion to the games.

The Procurator shook his head at her horror. "You will enjoy my victory in spite of it," he said confidently, "and everyone will enjoy you — the people will surround the lovely wife of the winner, rejoicing; and my Claudia will be celebrating victories far surpassing my own." He fell silent, amazed that this homage made so little impression upon her. "Can you really have forgotten how beautiful you are?" he asked in surprise. But this appeal also was without effect. "I fear for you," she whispered. He started, irritated at her words: "Fear, if I drive the chariot?"

"Not only if you drive the chariot," she replied. At this he looked at her strangely, tensely. For some moments it seemed as though a conversation long overdue,

23

was about to begin between them; but the Procurator with a peculiarly vehement gesture was already turning away, as though he could not endure the look in her eyes.

During the time that ensued, I repeatedly had the impression that he became impatient, irritated by her anxiety for him. Doubtless, he had found the coquettish little egoist of the past much more attractive. And yet it was only now that Claudia's beauty had fully unfolded; but oddly enough, it no longer affected him. Her eyes, especially, which he had formerly admired so much, left him cold. Even more, it almost seemed sometimes as though they made him uncomfortable. Furthermore, Claudia's beauty no longer made an impression upon society. Perhaps the reason lay in the fact that she no longer made use of the fashionable arts with which she formerly charmed the world. I always brought the creams and cosmetics to her conscientiously, and she was perfectly willing to use them; but she invariably forgot to do so when I did not remind her. "She adheres to the strict custom of our ancestors, she has no relationship with the living Rome," society would grumble when they saw her, her face having grown more and more soulful, as she sat pale and trembling beside her husband at the Circus.

That this living Rome was a new reality with which one had to make friends or come to an agreement, could certainly not be denied. At the time when we left it to go to Judea, the successor to the great Augustus was still reigning, and the glory of his name filled everyone with pride and confidence. This glory had vanished now, and terrible death sentences darkened the later times of Tiberius. In the Senate, men sought in vain for the bearers of familiar names. The Roman aristocracy had learned to die; but those who were spared knew how to live. It seemed almost as though the horrors through which they had passed helped them to an easier, a more carefree existence. No one in Rome alluded any longer to those darksome events; and the respected dead, those victims of criminal power, seemed to be forgotten. Amusing tales of scandal, questionable love adventures, above all, the successes in the arena absorbed all minds, and everyone seemed contented. In this attitude the Procurator was no exception. "Men are transitory; but the empire is eternal" he would say when occasionally these dead became the subject of conversation.

Only once I saw him momentarily frightened when

one of his freemen related with a scornful smile how, during the last days of the emperor, the cry rang throughout Rome: "Into the Tiber with Tiberius!" In Jerusalem we had once heard a similar cry; but I scarcely think, if the likeness between the two cries occurred to him at all, that the Procurator paid much attention to it. Besides how could he, although the parallel lay all too near, subject the Roman Empire, to him the greatest thing on earth, to such a comparison? We were hearing again about frightful murders in the imperial house and in the city. However, if the Procurator closed his eyes to the crimes of old Tiberius, he now seemed to consider it his duty even to defend the mad deeds of young Caligula.

"The welfare of the empire sometimes demands innocent victims," I heard him tell his wife; and I could not help thinking that it sounded as though he was defending himself.

"The welfare of the empire demands innocent victims," Claudia repeated tonelessly. Once more the conversation that had never taken place seemed to hover in the air.

"What do you mean? You wanted to say something," he said dubiously. Momentarily she crossed

26

her arms over her breasts, then as though with sudden decision, she took his hand and caressed it gently.

"Do you remember the time — ?" she began, her eyes large as they looked up at him.

"No," he interrupted, "I remember nothing." He turned away with vehemence. "Thanks be to the gods, I need know nothing more about Jerusalem!"

How did he come to mention Jerusalem? Not by a word had my mistress indicated that city — or did I imagine the name?

At such moments — I knew them by this time — I could never help feeling that her love wanted to force him to recollect something when it was not even certain that he was still able to do so. She was like a person who feels obliged to waken a sleeper and at the same time recoils at disturbing his rest. He sensed something of this. For a moment he would seem to be walking quickly and unsuspectingly toward a door that needed to be opened; but before reaching it, would turn back, confused but resolute. This impression I received many times and it gave me the feeling that inwardly he was slowly growing away from his wife.

The years passed without any evident change in the

relations between husband and wife. I do not know whether I had become accustomed to the tenseness in both or whether tenseness had relaxed with time. At any rate, Jerusalem was not mentioned any more. The conversation so frequently postponed, had still not taken place; but no one any longer expected it. The Procurator was growing elderly. A roll of flesh had formed under his strongly outlined chin, and the hot baths were not able to reduce his increasing weight. Like most Romans, he had become prematurely bald; therefore, according to the example of the great Caesar he usually appeared in public wearing a wreath of ivy or vine leaves. Claudia also, though many years younger, had faded; but her gentle expression of expectant seeking still left a breath of youthfulness upon her animated face.

With the years the Procurator had withdrawn more and more from her. His name was sometimes mentioned concerning other women. Claudia endured this as she had once endured the death of her child. I do not believe, however, that he ever stopped loving her and sometimes, strangely enough, I imagined that the thing apparently separating them was in reality a profound bond of union between them. Many were surprised that he did not dissolve his marriage with Claudia, since she had remained childless. Many even were surprised that Claudia herself did not insist upon her husband's divorce and remarriage in order to give him the happiness of having an heir. But so far as I know, this idea was never considered, doubtless an astonishing fact even when we remember that this marriage was one of the last still celebrated according to the old sacred rite, in presence of the Pontifex Maximus together with a sacrifice offered to Jupiter Capitolinus. Even such marriages, however, in the later period of Tiberius, were no longer indissoluble; and who under Caligula or Nero could still feel himself bound by the old gods?

Claudia also, with advancing years had turned more and more away from the gods to whom she was formerly attached with childlike trust. One might have believed that her husband's skepticism had infected her, and yet there was a world of difference. The Procurator was not in the least troubled by his godlessness, whereas Claudia was reduced to a state of profound restlessness such as affects persons who see their years slipping away without the expectation of their lives having been fulfilled.

29

I still remember one occasion when I accompanied her in her sedan chair across the forum. It was a radiant morning in spring, the temples and palaces were bathed in light. Never had the ancient sun shone upon anything so proud and lordly. You know, noble Julia, that I am otherwise a little reserved with regard to Roman buildings. In my native land they built more simply and therefore, according to my opinion, more nobly; but on that morning the glorious white marble with light upon it, made me involuntarily remember the foam of the sea. Like the goddess Aphrodite who rose from it, the goddess Rome was rising from her sea of whiteness. I mentioned this to my mistress; but she shook her head in protest. Thereupon a strangely impenetrable veil seemed to have dropped over her eyes. This transformation in the aspect of Rome, so distinctly visible to me, was it not for her also, the only change that had taken place? Was there something more in this city, some unknown cell from which a mysterious atmosphere had risen, something quiet, something powerful, that had not been before?

It was at this time that my mistress began to turn to the new cults which foreign merchants and legionaries had brought to the capital of the world. We sought out the temple of Cybele; I had to accompany her to the Egyptian mysteries of Isis, to those of the Syrian goddess, and those of Adonis and the Great Mother. Although at the beginning she devoted herself with great fervor to each of these deities in turn, it invariably happened that she turned away disillusioned and began her search anew. Finally she wished to be taken to the celebrated Sibyl of Tibur in order to learn the name of the divinity whose coming, as you know, she foretold to the great Augustus. Surely you still remember, noble Julia, the words which years ago circulated everywhere among the people: "From heaven will come the King of the Ages."

We therefore went to Tibur. The Sybil was an ancient woman who seemed entirely unaware of us as we entered the famous grotto. With closed eyes she was sitting in front of her hearth upon which apparently the fire was extinct, as was the life in the old woman's face. The grotto was growing dark like an entrance to the underground world. When I addressed the Sybil she did not answer. Probably she did not hear me, for the rushing of the waterfalls close at hand filled the room as though nature were trying to engulf the human voice. When my mistress silently touched the shoulder of the Sybil who sat submerged within herself the woman lifted her heavy head. From the coals on the hearth a sudden fire flamed, and it seemed as though two sister beings now recognized one another. Her eyes wide open, the old woman sat up and passed her quivering, ghost-like hand over the forehead and eyes of my mistress.

"Yes, I know, you too have seen Him," she murmured. "What more do you want of me? My time is over." Then suddenly her eyes paled as though struck by a strange, swift light, and her own face seemed taken from her. Foam came from her lips as it does when she prophesies. With a voice almost painfully loud, she cried out: "Go to the Subura, into the poorest house that you find — someone is there who knows more than I . . ." And then once more, heaving a deep and contented sigh: "My time is up . . . my world is gone. . . . "

Now you may imagine, noble Julia, that I did not readily find myself prepared for an evening walk into the Subura, that somewhat ill-famed section of the city where the little people make their purchases, where timid poverty and sometimes audacious crime house in tall tenement barracks. But my mistress would no longer let herself be dissuaded from going to the Subura, especially since she heard through one of our slaves of a new cult which was to have a meeting at an evening hour in one of the houses of that dismal quarter.

We consequently entered a miserable room which during the day may have served as a workshop for some small handicraftsman, and now accommodated a number of people. The slave girl who directed us to the place had given us the password by which they ·trustingly admitted us. I nevertheless persuaded my mistress to remain in the background; for the character of the small assembly made me a little uneasy. They were the poorest of the poor, many slaves among them and, unmistakably, several girls of the street. People of this type, when they know themselves in the majority, readily rise against those of higher position.

After a while, an old man in worn traveling clothes came in and knelt down in front of a simple table decked as for a ceremony. It was an altar, although we could see no manner of preparation for the sacrificing of the victim. The old man said a prayer; but because of his foreign accent we could not understand it too well. Thereupon he rose and asked those present to pray the Apostles' Creed together. Then something completely unexpected happened. At the bidding of the old man who was evidently the priest of this congregation, the assembly had risen. Timidly, apparently unpracticed for speaking in chorus, they answered the summons. They too spoke our language with a strongly barbarian intonation, so that we failed once more to grasp anything coherent. Suddenly I felt that Claudia Procula, beside me, was beginning to tremble violently. A dull feeling shuddered through me as though this poor, dimly lit room with its murmuring people were giving me a representation, an ominous repetition of a long forgotten event. Immediately, as though hurled aloft, breathless, from out of oblivion, the memory of my Lady's strange dream on that morning in Jerusalem, thrust itself upon me. Suddenly, with wondrously sharpened ears I caught the words: "Suffered under Pontius Pilate, was crucified, died, and was buried — "

Dispense me, noble Julia, from describing the effect that these words produced upon my mistress. She stood, as on that day upon the terrace of the Hall of Justice in Jerusalem, as though the lightning had struck her. But when I threw my arms around her

34

and tried gently to take her away, she tore herself vehemently from me and pressed her way impetuously toward the front. The praying chorus had ceased and the old traveling apostle began to speak: "I shall continue to preach to you the story of our Lord's Passion the climax of which we are approaching. The hearing before the Roman Procurator is over, and we shall continue with the account of our colleague in Jerusalem, who was an eye witness, and with his words give testimony to you, of the occurrence . . . 'and Pilate therefore . . . sat down on the judgment-seat at a place called Lithostrotos, but in Hebrew, Gabbatha. Now it was the Preparation Day for the Passover about the sixth hour. . . .' "

You know, honorable Julia, that thereafter we participated frequently in the meetings of the Nazarenes — the name that the little congregation in the Subura called itself — and soon we were attending regularly. You know that my mistress opened her heart to their message, while I upon hearing the Gospel of the Crucified, longed for the bright and beautiful gods of my native Greece. I also tried to influence my mistress by suggesting to her the thought that if the Condemned had truly come from heaven, He could have saved Himself from the snares of his enemies. "But He was from heaven," she replied quietly though firmly, "for He looked at His unjust judge with compassion." I could no longer contradict her; for this merciful glance had impressed itself also upon me like the greeting from an entirely different world, and I felt that it was this totally different thing that my mistress had been seeking in vain and now found at last.

And yet for her this discovery was linked with new and profound pain. She had accustomed herself to an attitude peculiarly her own, which gave expression to her sorrow. Never could she hear the Nazarenes' Confession of Faith without completely veiling her head at the name of Pontius Pilate. Likewise, despite her perfect surrender to her new belief, she did not dare to ask for baptism, the actual admission into the congregation; for she feared to arouse their aversion if she were to make herself known as the wife of Pontius Pilate. Nor did I venture to remove this fear which to me seemed justified. We therefore attended these meetings without revealing our identities, and no one seemed disquieted. The greeting "Maran atha, the Lord is coming" was sufficient for this friendly, inoffensive congregation to tolerate us in their midst.

36

Nevertheless, these simple people also were struck by the reserve and the grief of my mistress. Whenever the young assistant who, after the old apostle's departure directed the congregation, invited the newcomers to the preparation for baptism, he would look expectantly toward my mistress; but she, with a gesture of sorrow, always veiled her face.

Sometimes several members of the congregation would join us on the way home. Confidingly they opened their hearts to us and we saw to our astonishment that a great expectancy, not only otherworldly, but also of this world, burned within them. Among these was an old Syrian woman whose once beautiful features were now completely wasted. She was convinced that the fall of the unbelieving world was close at hand. With its fall the cruel games of the Circus would come to an end, wild animals would emerge from their cages and lie at men's feet, and gladiators would throw their swords away. The rich would divide their goods, masters would free their slaves, and above the Palatine of cruel Caesars the Dove of the Holy Spirit would appear. "Maran atha, Maran atha, Our Lord is coming!" she would cry. "Believe it, all of you; all of you be glad!" Then she would say to my

37

mistress, walking silently beside her: "And you, poor, sorrowing sister, you will be happy as a radiant young bride! Maran atha, Our Lord is coming!"

But the Lord did not come and bloody persecution followed. You know, noble Julia, about the fatal fire which at that time reduced some of the poorer quarters of Rome to rubbish and ashes, for which the innocent were made responsible in order to quiet the embittered population. One evening when we went to the dreary old tenement in the Subura again, we were for the first time halted at the door and asked for our names. Even then my mistress hesitated to mention hers. It was evident, however, that a totally different mood prevailed in the congregation. In looking about we found ourselves surrounded by frightened people who were staring at us with mistrust.

"What is your name? Why do you not tell us who you are?" we heard from all sides. "You make no effort to prepare yourself for baptism," they cried, turbulent with terror. "What do you really want among us?" Then the old Syrian woman pressed through the throng: "Be quiet, do be quiet, dear friends," she cried imploringly. "The Lord will come and protect us. Do not be anxious, the hairs of our head are counted — He who has said that, will not forsake us Maran atha, Our Lord is coming!"

At this point a man with a rough voice shouted at her: "Be still, old witch, it will be a long time before the Lord will come; but danger is coming!" Then he turned to Claudia: "Not another step until we know who you are and what you are looking for here!" The speaker, a gigantic Ethiopian slave, placed himself boldly before my mistress and barred the entrance to the house. She had become deadly pale; but remained silent — the noble Roman lady did not allow herself to be coerced. Meanwhile the tumult steadily increased. The Ethiopian seized my mistress by the shoulder and shook her: "I want to know your name, your name — you proud creature!"

At this moment of greatest distress, the Apostle's young assistant appeared. "What is going on here?" he called imperiously. "That which you commanded," the Ethiopian answered sullenly. "We asked an unknown woman her name; but she refuses to tell it!" The assistant, a serious young Roman, ordered the crowd to be quiet. "Let the woman go!" he said to the Ethiopian; then he turned to Claudia: "What is your name? Tell us your name."

"I will gladly tell it," she replied; "but to you alone." Without a word he let us enter a little side room. "Forgive the tumult," he said in his friendly manner. "Rumors are circulating through the city, which, it is to be hoped, cannot be confirmed; but these people feel themselves in danger — they are very weak, and you have never requested baptism. Until now we have not asked you why; but today it is imperative — we fear that we are being spied upon."

"Sir, I would gladly have requested baptism," she said simply, "but I did not dare to mention my name. I feared that it would frighten you — I am Claudia Procula — the wife of Pontius Pilate." At the name of the Procurator, the assistant started in surprise; but a moment later, something like joy shone in his face. "Your name does not frighten us, Claudia Procula," he replied. The Lord's disciple whom you heard preach, gave us the assurance that you warned your husband against pronouncing an unjust judgment. You have no part in his guilt, and can lift your head without shame when we say the Creed."

"Sir, let me continue to veil my face," she replied. "It is difficult for me to hear this Creed; for I am deeply attached to my husband. Can I not do penance for him, that his name may be blotted out of the Confession of Faith?"

The young Roman looked at her with a serious face. "No, Claudia Procula," he said in measured tones, "that, you cannot do. Whenever this Creed is recited the name of Pontius Pilate will also be spoken. With this name your husband once stood for the Roman Empire in Jerusalem, and therefore it remains for all time, in testimony of the place and the hour of the event."

Again the expression of sorrow gave soul to her face. Her voice grew ardent. "And yet," she said, "Our Lord meant him also when He prayed: 'Father, forgive them, for they know not what they do.'"

"But your husband knew what he was doing — you yourself had told him," the assistant replied, not without severity.

"But he did not understand me," she pleaded. "He did not recognize the mercy of God in the face of the Accused. And how could he recognize it — for in his world there is no mercy!"

"He knew, nevertheless, that he delivered an innocent Man to death," the assistant persisted. "Poor woman, I can give you no comforting answer. Your

husband is condemned, since he condemned the Lord
— and you are not in good faith if you resist the justice
of God. Let yourself be instructed in the Faith, and
you will understand."

She was silent for a while and slowly her gentle face
assumed an expression of firmness of purpose. Finally
she spoke, and her voice was low and solemn: "Farewell. I did not come here to seek the justice of God,
I came to seek the mercy of Christ, that which is not
of this world — the something totally different. But
you recognize it as little as my husband recognized it.
Not he alone, you too are guilty of the death of the
Lord — and at this moment you are guilty of it again;
for you are rejecting His divine mercy!"

For an instant the young assistant seemed struck;
but then an appallingly judicial look imprinted itself
upon his face. "What do you know, woman, of God's
justice? Do you want to instruct us, perhaps? You
who are not even baptized and never can be if you
persist in your error! Go now and think over my
words." He opened a side door again and let us out,
unobserved by the crowd.

The night was very dark; restless clouds hurried
across the moon. From time to time the errant flash

42

of a torch, carried by some outrider at the head of a nightly cavalcade, shone through the dim streets, casting a flickering light over the gloomy houses of the Subura. In these ancient buildings, long doomed to destruction, human beings were crowded together, according to the custom of centuries, living, sinning, finally dying, to give place to others who according to the same dull, monotonous customs, lived, sinned, and died. Off and on one could hear the roaring of wild animals from the distant amphitheater or the signals of the praetorian guards in the barracks. Women of the streets whisked by with impudent laughter.

My mistress walked very quickly, as though she could not make sufficient haste in leaving the Subura. I knew that she was inconsolable, but not by a single word did I dare to comfort her; for I felt her disillusionment as though it were my own. When at length we came to the region of the Emperor's fora, the moon had emerged from the clouds. Marble-white, the palatine rose before our eyes. Temple upon temple, strongholds of the ancient gods, lined the street through which we were walking. Once we were overtaken by a division of one of the legions. The even beat of their feet, like the iron rhythm of Rome, made the night

43

tremble. We were passing along the high wall of the temple of Mars Ultor when my mistress suddenly stood still while her hand groped its way up the cold stones.

"Mars Ultor," she whispered, "Mars the Avenger! O how firmly his house stands! And I was foolish enough to believe that it would fall! But it will never fall — nor will the Nazarenes overthrow it. Caesar will always triumph over Christ as he once triumphed over Him in Jerusalem. Again and again they will put barbarian princes to death on the Capitoline Hill and offer innocent animals as bloody victims to the gods. Again and again our legions will overthrow peaceful nations — again and again they will say: Woe to the conquered! Again and again they will cry: An eye for an eye and a tooth for a tooth! And if Christ should return today as the Syrian woman expected, even then nothing would change — they would nail Him to the cross again and everything would remain as it is. Not the totally different, but always the same thing comes and will come forever in this world. And if the Nazarenes would actually win this city and if every temple of the ancient gods were to be dedicated to Christ, the city would nevertheless remain what it is: not the city of Christ, but the city of Caesar.

"But perhaps," I ventured to interpose, "Christ would look upon this city as He once did upon His judge." She made no reply. I did not know whether she had not heard me or whether she did not wish to hear.

From then on we no longer attended the meeting of the Nazarenes, and although I saw how grievously my mistress suffered from this break, I was nevertheless glad; for the accusations circulating around Rome against the little community were becoming more numerous. The Procurator also for the first time found himself forced to take notice of this congregation. He had lately been suffering from an injury of the shoulder, the result of a fall during one of the chariot races for which, by reason of his age, he was no longer fitted. But you know, noble Julia, that it was one of the malicious amusements of young Emperor Nero to force even white-haired senators into the arena and to make sport of their awkwardness. The Procurator was the more unhappy at his defeat since he feared to have fallen into disgrace at the Palatine; for it was some time since any charge from the imperial palace had been given him.

A physician visited him daily to bandage the wound

and, in order to divert the patient from thinking of his condition, he supplied him with many items of news gleaned from his hurried visits from house to house. He happened to hear one day that a certain sect called Nazarenes were being held responsible for the burning of Rome. "Of course I regard them as quite harmless," said the doctor. "Imagine, Pontius Pilate, they believe in a certain Jesus of Nazareth, whom following the example of our Emperor cult, they have divinized. It is a question of a young dreamer who some thirty years ago was crucified in Jerusalem because He passed Himself off to the Jews as the Messias. You should really know more about Him since this must have happened while you were Procurator of Judea — "

The Procurator, bored by the conversation, shrugged his shoulders. The time was past when the remembrance of Judea still excited him. His distinguished Roman face did not move a muscle. Only the little cushion of flesh under his chin, which made him so unhappy, rose and fell slightly, as a result of his shortened breathing.

"I really do not remember any more, my friend," he replied absent-mindedly. "Those Jewish affairs were

46

always very unpleasant and I am no longer concerned about them."

" "Too bad!" The talkative doctor who certainly had hoped to learn more about the origin of the Nazarenes from the Procurator, turned to Claudia. "Does the mistress also no longer remember?" She and I, as usual, were prepared to help the doctor in bandaging the wound. The Procurator placed great value upon Claudia's presence. Since his illness, her nearness seemed to give him a sense of well-being. When the doctor addressed her, the instrument suddenly dropped from her hands. I picked it up and waited to return it to her; but she paid no heed.

"O yes," she faltered, "yes, I remember. It was when I dreamed — ." She stopped. I, too, held my breath. The long suppressed conversation, suddenly inevitable, was close at hand. Strangely enough, the Procurator was not aware of this — must I say 'no longer aware'? Had it really become too late for him to remember?

"What kind of dream was it?" her husband asked without suspicion.

"It was — a dream of warning," she stammered.

"And I, naturally, heeded your warning?" he said good-humoredly.

"No, you pronounced the sentence notwithstanding . . ." She fell silent. Evidently she felt herself hampered by the physician's presence, and the latter intruded himself into the conversation again:

"Did the lady's dream, perhaps, concern the One who was crucified?" he asked. "Then it must really have been you, Pontius Pilate, who condemned Him. I thought so at once — the time element points too distinctly to the fact. Do you still not remember?"

The Procurator looked distractedly down at his hands. From the bandaging of his wound several drops of blood had fallen upon them. I handed him a bowl of perfumed water and he dipped his hands into it. Suddenly he shuddered: "Alas yes, I remember dimly," he said. "The Jews once brought Someone to me, who regarded Himself as the Messias, and by Jupiter Capitolinus, this Man wore a strange expression! No one, before or since, has ever looked at me like that." He stopped short, avoiding the eyes of his wife. There was a moment of utter silence. Then, apparently undisturbed, Pilate continued.

"These Nazarenes, then, are being held responsible for the Roman conflagration? The Procurator turned once more to the doctor. "What an absurd idea!

Naturally, however, some attempt must be made to quiet the people."

"Yes, of course," the physician said. "They have already condemned several of these Nazarenes, who are said to have died very courageously, confessing their Faith to the end and forgiving their executioners — but what is wrong with the mistress?" he said interrupting himself, and jumping up. "Can I help you, Claudia Procula?"

She did not reply, but with swaying steps hurried from the room. I followed her. Outside, she threw herself sobbing into my arms.

"And I have condemned these people, exactly as they condemned my husband, and as he once condemned the Lord! Just exactly! But Christ has erected His sign over them — He has accepted them as His witnesses of blood! Yes, it is true: Christ is defeated always and everywhere, and He has been defeated also in me. They were right in refusing me baptism, O they were right!"

The Procurator in the meantime dropped the metal ball impatiently into the cymbal. I answered the summons and went in to quiet his fears concerning his wife's spell of faintness. He was accustomed to her

49

sensitivity and seemed no longer concerned about the outcome of the conversation. A few days later, however, he was reminded of it when an imperial command came which, under the pretext of uncovering the causes of the catastrophic Roman fire, charged him with carrying out the decree against the Nazarenes.

I thought that Claudia would be horrified; but she was only deeply moved when she heard of the imperial command. "God is very merciful," she said, "God is very merciful. He is confronting my husband again with the decision that once was his failure." She then sent me to Pilate with the request that he come to her room. I found him in excellent humor. The doctor had removed the bandage on the previous day, he felt himself restored, and, by reason of the emperor's assignment, relieved of the fear of having fallen into disgrace. The slave whom he had once had instructed in magic, was with him. The Procurator, after his fall in the chariot race, had banished him from his presence. I was surprised to see him again, this dusky person whose sly face in the background made me peculiarly uneasy today.

As usual, the Procurator listened to me courteously; but replied that his wife might await him in the atrium instead of in her room. That his wish ran counter to hers, was clear to me at once. To Claudia it was important to be alone with him, a situation which he, since the conversation in the doctor's presence, desired to avoid.

I returned to my mistress and we went over to the atrium together. The morning sun poured into the open place. The surrounding colonnade, as well as the little temple with the household gods, was in shadow; but the marble bench beside the fountain, where my mistress seated herself, stood in warming radiance. From distant streets the tumult of the populace, subdued yet louder than on other days, echoed into the stillness.

Considerable time elapsed before the Procurator appeared. The sedan chair which was to carry him to the Palatine was expected at any moment. The slave appointed for his service was already standing among the columns waiting with the luggage, close enough so that it was possible for him to overhear the conversation. From moment to moment other servants slipped busily by. The Procurator who had counted upon this semipublicity, detained me firmly when I wanted to leave. He found himself disappointed, however; for to Claudia the presence of others did not make the slightest difference. She did not even notice it. Much too profoundly conscious of the meaning of this hour for which she had hoped and waited for years, this tender, silent woman was altogether oblivious of the fact that she was not alone with her husband.

Quietly she listened to his words of farewell; but then went straight to her goal. Softly, but very firmly she said: "I entreat you earnestly, my husband, return your appointment to the emperor. Have nothing to do with the persecution of these Nazarenes, do not lend yourself again to the condemnation of the innocent." The Procurator did not seem surprised at Claudia's strange request; for in a single instant the whole situation in its shocking recurrence lay clear before his mental vision.

"Really, I have nothing against these little sects," he said quietly. "Of what concern are the Nazarenes to me? For a Roman, Rome is all that matters, and Rome is the imperial will. The Palatine has informed me that these people are incendiaries. It is said, furthermore, that they refuse the obligation of sacrifice to the emperor. They are consequently to be regarded as rebels."

"They are no more rebels than was He whose name they bear," she replied, with the same gentle assurance.

He knew at once to whom she referred. "Nevertheless," he said, "He was under the suspicion of wanting to make Himself king. He Himself admitted it to me."

"But His kingdom is not of this world," she replied.

"He also said that at the time; but what was I to think? A kingdom that is not of this world! Who knows such a kingdom?"

"He who is of the truth." Was this Claudia's voice speaking? — How strange this almost literal repetition!

The Procurator shrugged his shoulders. "What is truth? Our philosophers would be happy if they could tell us. Do you, perhaps, know more than they?"

"I know that you did not know who He was upon whom you pronounced sentence. . . ." Her voice was now of the utmost intensity. "Yes, He was and is a King: the King of the Ages, whom the Sybil of Tibur foretold to Augustus."

At these words a sudden terror seemed to come upon him — the last dike had given way: the never forgotten, the unforgettable, broke with force from the depths of his being. "How can you say," he cried, "that I condemned Him? It was the Jews who forced

53

me to give Him up. I defended His innocence to the end — I left nothing undone to save Him. Did I not for His sake make friends with that miserable fox, Herod, in the hope that as His sovereign he might be able to free Him? Did I not try by the scourging of their Victim to satisfy the Jewish hyenas? Did I not set up the murderer Barabbas as a choice to force them to ask for the liberation of this Jesus? I maintained to the end that I believed Him innocent, and I washed my hands before all the world, that this Blood might not descend upon me! Go to the Jews; they have taken it upon themselves — what is it that you want of me? With what are you reproaching me? With what have you reproached me all these years, when you fixed your eyes upon me with your unbearable look, with the look that has ruined our happiness?" He clenched his hands. Was it anger? Was it fear? "What do you want to tell me with that look?"

She took one step toward him and opened her arms wide. "That I have compassion for you, my Beloved." It was all that she said; but she put both her arms around him and drew his head to her breast. I could not recognize her face, nor his. I recognized only the primeval utterance of love uplifted to that compassion which once, before the tribunal in Jerusalem, seemed to embrace the world. Nothing remained between these two human beings except that which had not been and never could be destroyed. Guilt and love had found one another.

Moments passed while neither spoke. "Claudia, my Claudia," Pilate said at last, in a voice that was scarcely audible. Then after a while, more distinctly: "What do you know of those for whom you are pleading?"

Had her compassion won the victory? From the street rose an ugly noise, which for some time had been drawing nearer and nearer until we could hear the cry: "To the lions with the Nazarenes! To the lions! Whosoever spares the criminals is not Caesar's friend!"

The Procurator started as though from a dream — his face grew dark. At that moment the slave who, unobserved, had been gradually approaching, announced that the sedan chair was ready.

And now, noble Julia, I must confess once more and with deep sorrow, my own remissness with regard to Claudia, of which I already told you in a former letter. To me it will always remain inconceivable that I failed to recognize it as the most logical thing in the world that Claudia, after having found her way inwardly back to those of her own faith, would join their congregation again. She would necessarily feel an even stronger desire now, to hurry to the Subura to give warning to those in danger. Perhaps she also believed that as the wife of the Procurator her presence might protect them. All this was inevitable; and yet, her preparations, which she made with great secrecy, were kept from me. She naturally did not want to draw me into a possible catastrophe, nor on the other hand did she wish to be hindered by me in carrying out her plan.

After the upsetting conversation with her husband, she withdrew to her room, asking me at the same time to leave her alone. With my lack of suspicion — a lack which seems incredible now — I was not aware of her disappearance until evening when I went to undress her for the night. I did not find her in her room, although it seemed strangely filled with her personality. Quite involuntarily I thought of her blissful awakening on that long past morning of her early married life. It was evening now, and in the growing darkness of her room the small statue of Eros which her husband had once given her, stood forsaken. Distracted, as though a loved person had gone forever, I stood upon the threshold. Was not the gracious love god of my native land also the god of death — into whose hand the great Praxiteles placed the lowered torch? My eyes fell upon the little three-legged bronze table beside Claudia's deserted couch. Upon it lay the small wax tablet which she used for the daily recording of household affairs. I picked it up and read the lines: "I am going in order to save my husband from a second crime. Be comforted, my Praxedis, if I should not return." Horror-struck, I let the tablet fall. Where had she gone, never to return? It must be the Subura. Immediately I hurried to find her, feeling that already I was too late.

Rome lay in darkness, like Jerusalem at the hour of the Crucifixion. In the Subura the shrill laughter of the women of the streets was hushed, and no human being passed me. Some deadly terror weighed heavily upon the entire region. The house of the Nazarenes lay still as a grave in the depths of the night. The door was shattered. Within yawned complete desolation. Breathlessly, I felt my way through to the assembly room; its door also stood open. Black, lonely night seemed to stare at me. Then I heard the sound

57

of despondent sobbing coming from a corner of the room. I felt my way toward it and found a dark figure lying on the floor. It was the Syrian woman. Tremblingly I touched her shoulder and spoke to her. Through the darkness she recognized my voice.

"It is all over," she faltered, "it is all over! The Lord did not come; the legionaries came — it is over — it is over forever!" She continued to lament, and only gradually I succeeded in getting her to tell me what had happened.

Claudia, as I suspected, had appeared at the meeting. The Syrian woman, true to her childlike confidence in the Lord's return in the extreme need of His people, had hidden herself that she might give the awaited One the first welcome. Thus she escaped arrest. From her hiding place she had seen how Claudia faced the legionaries when they arrived, and as the wife of Pontius Pilate, called upon them to give the prisoners their freedom. They mocked and ridiculed her and finally led her away with the others. Whither? Into prison? To death? The Syrian woman could give no answer.

I hurried home, sent messengers to the Procurator to tell him of Claudia's capture and beg him to rescue her; but the Procurator was not to be found. Meanwhile dismal rumors went straying through the city: my mistress, it was said, had been betrayed as a Nazarene by one of her husband's slaves. The Procurator also was reported to have fallen into disgrace with the emperor. In despair I sent out my Lady's favorite slave, but he never returned. Days of torture passed; until at last an unknown Nazarene brought me a letter. It was in Claudia's handwriting. I broke the seal and read:

"Written in prison, a few hours before receiving the Baptism of Blood.

"Greeting, blessing, and comfort to my beloved Praxedis! It was as God willed, and will be as God wills: no one can escape the mercy of Christ. Again God has visited me in a dream as He once visited me in Jerusalem. Once more I went through the temples and churches of the centuries — they had grown old and gray as a dying generation becomes old and gray. An abysmal sadness was within me, not because they had condemned me to death, but because I thought that I must die in vain; for was not my whole life and love but one repeated failure? All these churches seemed to me to be built upon a deceptive ground of faith, since the mercy of Christ could never triumph upon this earth. With the world as it is, that mercy could only break itself upon it. I ran from one temple to the other, trying to get into the open air. There was no end to them; but their structure grew more and more barren, more and more meaningless as though the builders knew only how to repeat outworn forms in which the soul no longer dwelt.

"But suddenly this picture changed: I arrived at a place which seemed even more strange than those through which I had passed. The walls were of material unknown to me, the room was wide open and bare; but light was streaming through it. Upon an altar there was nothing but the cross, the symbol of death! A dense, frightened multitude had pressed into this space, a choir was singing the Apostles' Creed: again my husband's loved name resounded, no longer now like a mounting accusation and a threat; but rather as though the voices as a last comfort were clinging to the words: Crucifixus etiam pro nobis sub Pontio Pilato. I heard at the same time a distant droning as though unprecedented storms had descended upon the land and were approaching rapidly.

"The walls of the temple in which I found myself,

swayed. Once more the cosmic chorous thundered my husband's name. Was this the end of all time? My foot halted as before untrodden ground. I felt the centuries ripping apart like a chain that had rotted. The last wall of the temple gave way and opened the view — into eternity! I saw coming in the clouds, a chair, the same chair that once stood before the Hall of Justice in Jerusalem. Upon it sat, not my husband, but He whom my husband had once condemned, and before Him — there where once the condemned had stood, my husband was standing awaiting his sentence. The One in the chair, however, gazed at him with the same glance of compassion, as once He had done in Jerusalem. At that moment I heard a voice: 'Be of good heart, Claudia Procula. I am the One totally different, whom you have constantly been seeking. I am the One who triumphed when overcome. I am the Source, the Abandonment, and the Triumph of Eternal Love — therefore be not afraid. You will die the same death as I. You will die for the salvation of the one who is letting you die.' "

Stunned and shaken, I dropped the page. For the first time in my life, the Faith of Christ had touched the depths of my soul.

At this moment the door burst open and the Procurator rushed headlong into the room. Was it really
he? Was this pain-tortured face, distorted with scorn,
that of our self-contained master? A Roman? Here
every mark of Roman dignity was gone. Only a human
being overcome by despair could have looked like this!

Like a tree that the ax had felled, he threw himself·
down beside the bed of my mistress. He tore the
wreath from his forehead, and with clenched fists beat
his breast.

"I have killed her, I have killed her," he cried over
and over. I stood as though frozen. I noticed then,
that Claudia's favorite slave had followed him. His
face, too, was bloodless to the lips.

"He — saw our mistress — die," the slave stammered.
"The emperor, that monster, betrayed him! He sat in
the Circus beside the emperor who feasted upon his
horror when, with the other Nazarenes, my mistress
entered the arena. They did not cry like the gladiators:
'Morituri te salutant' — those who are about to die
salute you; they prayed the Confession of their Faith.
I can still hear their last words: 'Crucifixus etiam pro
nobis sub Pontio Pilato — '" Crucified for us under
Pontius Pilate.

At the sound of his name, the Procurator looked up from where he knelt beside his wife's bed: "Slave, give me the sword," he groaned. "Quickly, quickly," he cried out when the trembling slave hesitated, "I cannot wait for death!" And rising to his feet he tore the weapon from him.

But then I grasped his hand, the one which was ready to strike. With power not my own, I said: "Pontius Pilate, Claudia died as Christ died — through you. But she died as He died — for you. He turned his distorted face toward me. With distraught eyes he looked at me long and without comprehension. Suddenly his glance lowered as though turning inward. The sword dropped from his hands.

Excuse me, noble Julia, from any added word. My story is ended. I, too, have been stricken by the look of the Crucified.

Also by Gertrud von le Fort

The
Eternal Woman

"At long last, after twenty years of waiting and wondering we have this *tremendous* book in English . . . there is such a wealth of wisdom and inspiration for anyone who is ready to think while reading, that one may hope for a real impact of the book on the actual condition of the American woman."   — *Worship*

"This is an unusual, a unique book, written with candor and deep spiritual insight."
    — *Catholic Library World*

". . . a stimulating treatise on symbolism, with emphasis on woman as symbol . . . deserves to be widely read and pondered."   — *Commonweal*

$3.50

THE WIFE OF PILATE
By Gertrud von le Fort
Bruce — $1.75

Lightning Source UK Ltd.
Milton Keynes UK
UKHW022107160223
417164UK00019B/145